This book is donated
by
Victoria Waterhouse
in celebration of
her 6th birthday

February 1999

For James, with love.
C. W. M.

*In memory of my mother
who taught me how to waltz one night
under a full moon.*
M. W.

*From both of us,
thank you Jack and Pat.*
C. W. M & M. W.

Text © 1998 by Constance W. McGeorge.
Illustrations © 1998 by Mary Whyte. All rights reserved.
Book design by Laura Jane Coats. Typeset in Goudy Oldstyle and Charlemagne.
The illustrations in this book were rendered in watercolor. Printed in China.
Library of Congress Cataloging-in-Publication Data
McGeorge, Constance W.
Waltz of the scarecrows / by Constance W. McGeorge ; illustrated by Mary Whyte.
p. cm.
Summary: While staying with her grandparents on their farm,
Sarah discovers the secret behind the local tradition of dressing the
scarecrows in formal gowns and fancy coats.
ISBN 0-8118-1727-X
[1. Scarecrows—Fiction.] I. Whyte, Mary, ill. II. Title.
PZ7.M478467Wa1 1997 [E]—dc21 97-1347 CIP AC

Distributed in Canada by Raincoast Books
8680 Cambie Street, Vancouver, British Columbia V6P 6M9

10 9 8 7 6 5 4 3 2 1

Chronicle Books
85 Second Street, San Francisco, California 94105

Web Site: www.chronbooks.com

WALTZ
OF THE
SCARECROWS

by Constance W. McGeorge ❧ illustrated by Mary Whyte

chronicle books·san francisco

Sarah awoke with a start. A loud noise shook the ceiling above her head. She threw back the quilt, jumped into her overalls, and was heading for the attic when she heard Grandma calling her downstairs for breakfast.

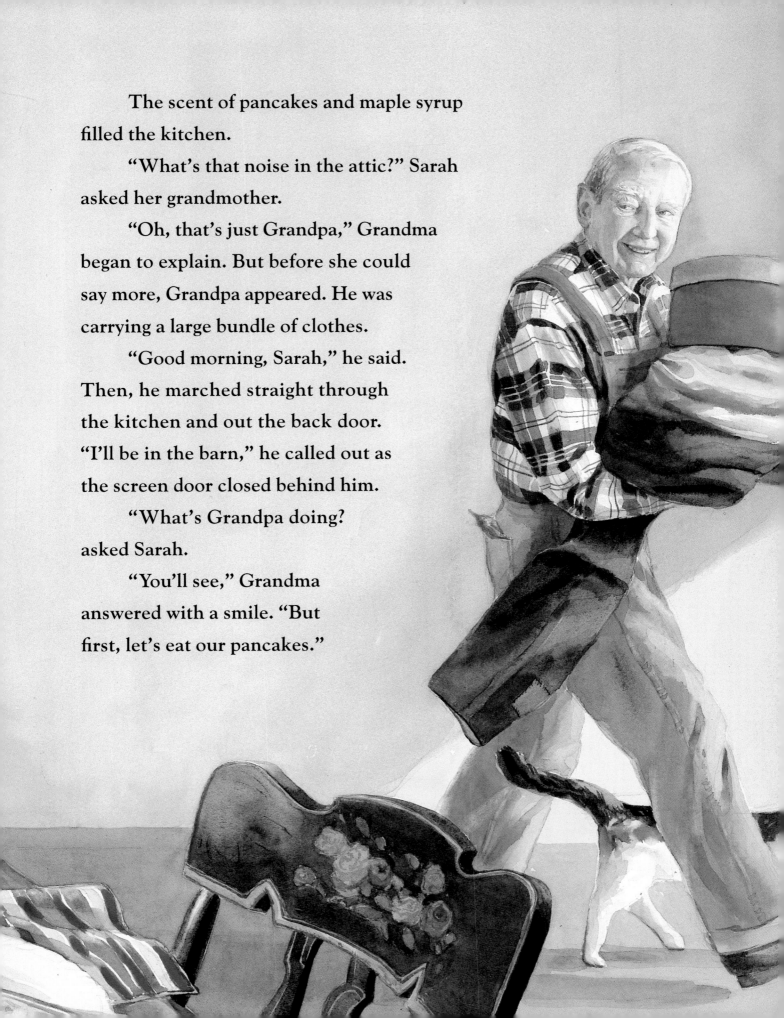

The scent of pancakes and maple syrup filled the kitchen.

"What's that noise in the attic?" Sarah asked her grandmother.

"Oh, that's just Grandpa," Grandma began to explain. But before she could say more, Grandpa appeared. He was carrying a large bundle of clothes.

"Good morning, Sarah," he said. Then, he marched straight through the kitchen and out the back door. "I'll be in the barn," he called out as the screen door closed behind him.

"What's Grandpa doing? asked Sarah.

"You'll see," Grandma answered with a smile. "But first, let's eat our pancakes."

Sarah hurried through breakfast then found Grandpa in the barn. He was sorting through the bundle of clothes from the attic.

Sarah watched him carefully unfold a man's evening coat with tails. Shaking out the wrinkles, he laid the coat down gently. Then, he straightened the brim of a shiny top hat. Next, he unwrapped a blue satin gown.

The sleeves of the coat were patched, and the gown had faded from a dark indigo to a sun-bleached blue. But still, they were the most beautiful clothes Sarah had ever seen.

"Sarah, my dear," Grandpa announced, "the crops are full and harvest is near—it's time to make scarecrows!"

"But I thought scarecrows only wore raggedy old clothes," said Sarah.

"Not *our* scarecrows!" answered Grandma. With her sewing basket in hand, Grandma sat down on a milking stool and set to work mending a tear in the faded blue gown.

Grandpa untied a bale of straw and began stuffing the old clothes. Sarah helped, buttoning buttons and filling sleeves and gloves with straw. Then, she and Grandma braided yarn for hair and sewed it around faces made of old pillow cases.

Finally, Grandma placed the top hat on the head of one scarecrow, and Sarah placed a hat with silk flowers on the head of the other.

As Sarah helped Grandma and Grandpa carry the scarecrows into the cornfield, she noticed a pair of scarecrows in the field across the road. One was wearing a black topcoat and the other a bright red ball gown. In the neighbor's garden, she saw another pair of scarecrows dressed in fancy clothes, too.

"Grandpa," Sarah cried, "all the scarecrows are dressed up!"

Grandpa sat down on an old tree stump and motioned to Sarah to sit beside him. "Why, it's a tradition here," he said. "It all started one summer long ago."

"That year, we had the best crops we'd ever seen. The corn grew a foot taller than usual, and there were more pumpkins on the vines than we could count. Even the sunflowers were brighter that year than anyone could remember.

"To celebrate our bounty, a harvest ball was planned. Folks sent away to the city for fancy clothes—evening coats and top hats, ball gowns and high-heeled shoes. The town was decorated with garlands and lanterns, and an orchestra came all the way from Riverton to play.

"At dusk, on the night of the ball, we dressed up in our fine new clothes and strutted into town. We were so excited, we didn't even notice the dark cloud approaching from the west. As the orchestra began to play and we started to dance, the cloud came closer and closer.

"As it turned out, it wasn't a dark cloud
at all. It was a swarm of hungry birds, and they
were after our crops!

"Screeching and cawing, the birds picked
at the corn, pulled at the beans, and poked at the
pumpkins. The orchestra stopped playing, and we
ran into the fields, shouting and shaking our fists.

"Well, those birds took one look at our black coats flapping and our colorful dresses billowing, and they took flight back into the evening sky!

"We must have been a sight, running through the fields, our fancy clothes flashing in the twilight. Luckily, our food for the coming year was saved. But worry was on everyone's mind. What would we do if the birds returned?

"Without a word, we knew what
we had to do. We hurried home and
changed into work shirts and overalls.
We cleaned our coats and mended our
gowns, and then we stuffed them all with straw.

"One by one, under the rising moon, the fanciest
scarecrows anyone had ever seen began to appear in
the fields. And, do you know what? The birds stayed
away. And they have stayed away every year since,"
Grandpa concluded.

"But there's more to the story," said Grandma,
her voice nearly a whisper. Sarah moved closer to hear
every word.

"Some folks say that when the crops are full and the harvest moon rises in the sky, a wind blows in from the south. The cornstalks sway, and the faint sound of music drifts through the fields.

"Others say they've heard the sounds of rustling satin, coattails flapping, and a shuffling that lasts long into the night."

"There are even a few," Grandpa added, "who claim they've *seen* the scarecrows waltzing."

Then, Grandpa and Grandma took
Sarah by the hand, and together they
twirled around and around.

One night, after Sarah had returned home from her summer visit to Grandpa and Grandma's farm, she sat at her bedroom window. Outside leaves rustled on the trees, and the full moon hung low in the sky. Sarah had an idea.

She opened the closet and took out her old velvet party dress. Just then, a soft knock sounded at her bedroom door. Her mother peeked in.

"This dress is too small for me," said Sarah. "I'm going to send it to Grandma and Grandpa."

"What are your grandparents going to do with an old party dress?" asked her mother.

Sarah smiled. She knew Grandma and Grandpa would know just what to do.